Helen Oxenbury
PIG TALE

First published in Great Britain 1973
by William Heinemann Ltd
Published 1990 by Little Mammoth
This edition 1998 by Mammoth
an imprint of Egmont Children's Books
Michelin House, 81 Fulham Road, London SW 3 6 R B

10 9 8 7 6 5 4 3 2 1

Text and illustration copyright © 1973 Helen Oxenbury
Helen Oxenbury has asserted her moral rights
Layout and design by Jan Pienkowski and Moira Ryan

ISBN 0 7497 0272 9

A CIP catalogue record for this title is available from the British Library

Printed in the U.A.E. by Oriental Press Ltd.

This is the story of two bored pigs.
She was called Bertha and his name was Briggs.
They would lie in the grass and moan and complain:
"Nothing happens to us – every day is the same!"

They had plenty to eat,

a warm sty with a thatch,

An orchard to play in

and trees for a scratch,

Cool mud for a wallow,

fields full of flowers,

Soft turf for a doze

or gossip for hours.

But Bertha and Briggs were never content.
On money and riches their two minds were bent.
There were so many wonderful things they would do –
Only then would they really be happy, they knew.

Then one sunny day they were nosing about
When Briggs grubbed up a chest with the end of his snout.
They opened the lid with a squeal of delight,
For the chest contained treasure, all glittering bright.

"We are rich!" they cried
out as they cleaned
themselves down,

And clutching the chest
they set off for the town.

The noise of the traffic
alarmed the two pigs

And Bertha clung tight
to the trotter of Briggs.

Briggs was soon dreaming
of shiny new cars

While Bertha gazed into
shop windows for hours.

They came to a bank and
looked shyly about

Till the manager angrily
ordered them out.

He ordered them out – then he noticed the box,
And his eyes had a gleam like a wily old fox.
Briggs lifted the lid of the treasure so rare –
The manager gasped and said "Well, I declare!"
He bowed and he scraped and he said with a purr:
"Won't you please take a seat now, dear madam and sir?
I will give you some cash, Mr Briggs, if I may:
You will find it is simpler than jewels when you pay."
He locked up the treasure behind a steel door
And gave them a case stuffed with banknotes galore.
"Thank you, oh thank you!" said Bertha with glee.
"Come Briggs, let us start on our great shopping spree."

They went to a large and luxurious store
Where Bertha bought dresses and hats by the score.

Briggs' turn was next, and he felt quite a swell –
He tried on four suits and they fitted him well.

From the store to the showrooms was not very far
So they hurried to buy an expensive new car.

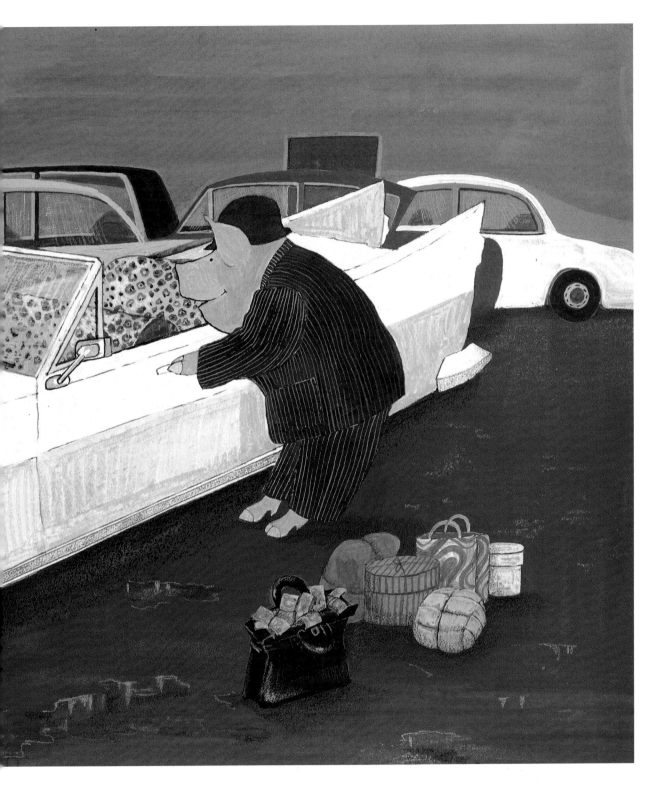

"This model's the latest," the car salesman said.
"Then I'll have it!" cried Briggs, feeling light in the head.

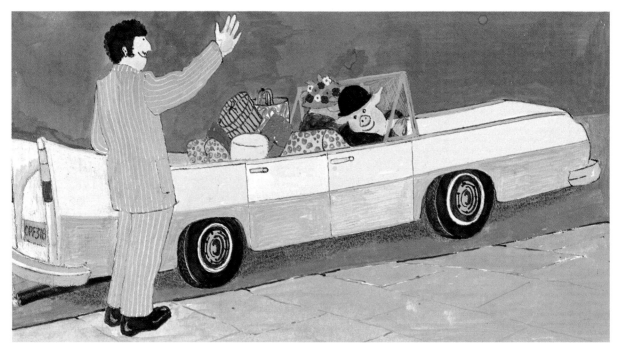

In jumped the two pigs, and they sped on their way
To purchase a house by the end of the day.

They went to an agent who handed to Briggs
Some pictures of houses just right for two pigs.

Bertha soon spotted the house with most charm –
The one she had seen from the gate on the farm.

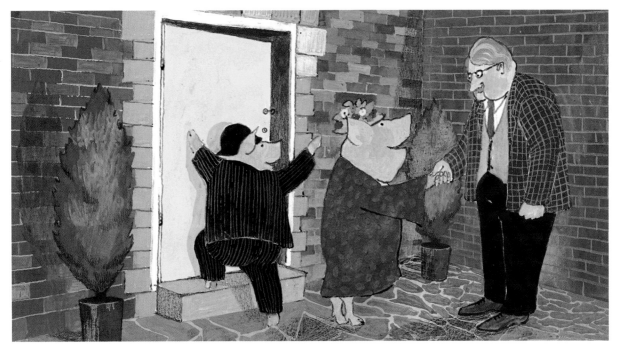

The agent escorted them both to the door,
Then left them alone to go in and explore.

That night they were happy as two pigs could be
And they talked and they planned until well after three,

But tossing and turning 'twixt blankets and sheet
Poor Briggs hardly slept on account of the heat.

Bertha made breakfast,

Briggs pottered about.

He polished the car,

she cleaned the house out.

Bertha cooked dinner

while Briggs sat and read.

He made a few phone calls,

watched telly till bed.

One day, feeling restless with nothing to do,
While Bertha was busy preparing a stew,
Briggs drove his new car through the green countryside,
Speeding down lanes that were not very wide.
Suddenly out of the engine there shot
A cloud of black smoke and of steam boiling hot.
The car gave a cough and a lurch and a leap,
Then rolled to a halt near a flock of white sheep.
Briggs lifted the bonnet and prodded around,
But the cause of the trouble just could not be found.
The longer he struggled the crosser he got,
Till at last, in despair, very tired and too hot,
He threw down the spanner and uttered a moan –
He'd just have to start on the long walk back home.

When he opened the door Briggs instantly knew
That Bertha's new gadgets were troublesome too.

"Oh Briggs," Bertha sobbed, "what a miserable day!
I've been working so hard I've had no time to play."

From that moment on

nothing seemed to go right.

House, garden and pigs

were a terrible sight.

At last the two pigs

couldn't stand any more.

Briggs grabbed Bertha's arm

and they dashed through
the door.

From the garden they gazed at the country beyond
And Briggs in a rage pushed his car in the pond.
They felt no regrets as they ran through the gate
And away from the life they had soon grown to hate.
They pulled off their clothes and ran on faster still,

Didn't even look back as they tore up the hill.
Breathless they ran through the old orchard gate –
For a roll in the mud the two pigs couldn't wait.
To be careless and free and to romp and to play
Was all that they wanted to do every day.

That night as they lay gazing up at the sky
Bertha and Briggs heaved a rapturous sigh.
"Let's stay here for ever," said Bertha to Briggs,
And they fell fast asleep, two tired happy pigs.